Ladybird I'm Ready...
for Phonics!

Note to parents, carers and teachers

Ladybird I'm Ready for Phonics is a series of phonic reading books that have been carefully written to give gradual, structured practice of the synthetic phonics programme your child is learning at school.

Each book focuses on a set of phonemes (sounds) together with their graphemes (letters). The books also provide practice of common tricky words, such as **the** and **said**, that cannot be sounded out.

The series closely follows the order that your child is taught phonics in school, from initial letter sounds to key phonemes and beyond. It helps to build reading confidence through practice of these phonics building blocks, and reinforces school learning in a fun way.

Ideas for use

- Children learn best when reading is a fun experience. Read the book together and give your child plenty of praise and encouragement.

- Help your child identify and sound out the phonemes (sounds) in any words she is having difficulty reading. Then, blend these sounds together to read the word.

- Talk about the story words and tricky words at the end of each story to reinforce learning.

For more information and advice on synthetic phonics and school book banding, visit **www.ladybird.com/phonics**

Book Band 2

Level 5 builds on the sounds learnt in levels 1 to 4 and introduces new sounds and their letter representations:

j   v   w   x   y   z   zz   qu

Special features:

repetition of sounds
in different words

short sentences with
simple language

Vick has to visit Zelda.
She has a bad leg.

Liz and Vick get Zelda
into a pen.

We did it!

22

23

Story Words

Can you match these words
to the pictures below?

Vick

Liz

The Canyon

Zelda

Nutmeg

bucket

liquid

wet

30

Tricky Words

These tricky words are in the story
you have just read. They cannot
be phonetically sounded out. Can
you memorize them and read them
super fast?

the   to

into   we

she   be

he

31

summary page
to reinforce learning

Written by Monica Hughes
Illustrated by Ian Cunliffe

Phonics and Book Banding Consultant: Kate Ruttle

A catalogue record for this book is available from the British Library

Published by Ladybird Books Ltd
80 Strand, London, WC2R 0RL
A Penguin Company

001

ISBN: 978-0-72327-541-1
Printed in China

Ladybird I'm Ready... for Phonics!

Jazz the Vet

Zac and his dad visit
Jazz the vet.

Zac's rabbit has a bad leg.

Jazz picks up the rabbit
and rubs his leg.

Jazz tells Zac he can fix the leg. The rabbit gets a jab into the top of his leg.

Val visits the vet. She has a big red parrot. The parrot yells at Jazz.

Jazz has to be quick.
The parrot will nip him.

A man has a big bag.
He unzips the bag.
It has seven kittens in it!

The kittens get jabs and
a tub of pills.

Jazz has to put the kittens back into the bag but he has six kittens, not seven!

A kitten was in a big box.
She had a nap!

Story Words

Can you match these words to the pictures below?

Zac

Dad

Jazz

rabbit

parrot

kitten

bag

Tricky Words

These tricky words are in the story you have just read. They cannot be phonetically sounded out. Can you memorize them and read them super fast?

the

he

into

she

to

be

me

was

Ladybird I'm Ready... for Phonics!

Vick the Vet

Vick is a vet. She gets into a van to visit Liz.

Liz runs The Canyon.

Vick has to visit Zelda.
She has a bad leg.

Liz and Vick get Zelda into a pen.

Vick picks up the leg.
The leg has a cut on it.

Vick tells Liz she will fix
the leg.

Vick dabs the cut and puts
a pad on it.

Liz tells Vick she has
to visit Nutmeg.

He is sick.

Vick gets a big pill.
She has to mix it into
the liquid in a bucket.

Nutmeg sucks up the liquid.
He will be well.

Vick is wet, wet, wet!

Story Words

Can you match these words to the pictures below?

Vick

Liz

The Canyon

Zelda

Nutmeg

bucket

liquid

wet

Tricky Words

These tricky words are in the story you have just read. They cannot be phonetically sounded out. Can you memorize them and read them super fast?

the

to

into

we

she

be

he

Collect all
Ladybird I'm Ready... for Phonics!

Captain Comet's Space Party

9780723275374

Nat Naps!

9780723275381

Top Dog

9780723275398

Huff! Puff! Run!

9780723275404

Fix It Vets

9780723275411

Dash is Fab!

9780723275428

Say the Sounds

9780723271598

Flashcards

9780723272069

Ladybird I'm Ready for... apps are now available on iPad, iPhone and iPod touch.

Apps also available on Android devices